CONNIE'S WEDDING

A NIGHT STALKERS WEDDING STORY

3 8-11-18

M. L. BUCHMAN

Buchman Bookworks

SIGN UP FOR M. L. BUCHMAN'S
NEWSLETTER TODAY

8-11-18 #3

and receive:
Release News
Free Short Stories
a Free Novel

Do it today. Do it now.
www.mlbuchman.com/newsletter

Other works by M. L. Buchman:

CHAPTER 1

FIVE YEARS AGO

"Who were you?"

"What are you talking about?"

Connie sat in the stopped car and waved helplessly out the windshield.

"Who was I?" Big John dominated the right seat of the rental car—he was broad-shouldered and tall enough to dominate any car, but this one was a squeeze. He squinted out the front windshield as if searching for a clue. Something Connie was lacking at the moment.

"No, I mean who was *I?*"

"Being even less clear than usual, Connie. And that's saying something, girl. You're Sergeant Connie Davis and I'm Sergeant John Wallace. We're getting married in two days. Pleased to meet you." He held out a hand as if to shake hers. Instead she grabbed onto it with both of hers and held on.

He was right, her thoughts were usually clarified and tested inside her head before she gave voice to them. Only around John did she ever let that barrier down. She'd try again.

"Six months ago, I was here at your farm for three days. It

1

didn't look anything like this." The previously winter-barren Oklahoma fields now stretched out of view with wheat to the left and corn to the right. She'd never imagined that the four tall trees at the four corners of the cozy two-story farmhouse would be massively pink magnolias in mid-June. The wrap-around porch was embraced by roses in a thousand shades. "It all looks so...homey."

"It is home. That's why it looks that way. And we'd be there if you'd just drive that last couple hundred feet."

"But who was I then? I...ran away."

She'd left abruptly six months ago in the middle of a devastating loss for the family. Grandpa Wallace, Grumps, had died. And, not knowing what else to do, she had walked away.

No, she'd run.

Had she thought she was protecting the family by removing the obvious outsider? She certainly hadn't recognized that there was any more than sex between her and John. It wouldn't be until she was barfing out her guts from pure terror against the sides of the Stockholm Cathedral that she'd come to understand that.

Had she thought she was protecting her heart by running away? Instead, she'd run from the only man who recognized she had one. Another thing she hadn't understood at the time.

Instead she had wounded the man she'd been learning to love—the first ever in her life. Thankfully, John had forgiven her.

But would the rest of his family? Their texts said yes, but her heart—and nerves—were far less sure. They were now just a hundred feet down the gravel driveway and she didn't recognize it at all. The tall corn blocked her view of the barn where she'd rebuilt Grumps' tractor. The house and its massively blooming trees blocked the view of the orchard around back.

The only thing that made sense to her in the entire vista was John close beside her and looking worried.

She hadn't seen a single one of the family since that day she'd run, except for Big John of course. Their team had been deployed in Eastern Europe—on the types of missions that no one in Eastern Europe could ever know about. They had been working to delay the Russian expansion, but it was clear that they were gearing up to roll westward once more. It looked as if Ukraine and Syria were in their sights and there was only so much the Night Stalkers could do to slow them down—warning Ukraine of the dangers to their Crimea region was still proving pointless. Some missions had delivered pinpoint "insurgency" at critically tactical moments. Dozens of other raids had gathered intel that the Russians had fought to hide.

The drastic setbacks they'd delivered to the Russian Navy's plans to create a new fleet of aircraft carriers could also never be pinpointed to the Night Stalkers of the 160th SOAR.

Sergeant Connie Davis recognized herself as Connie the soldier. She was proud of the silent, fanatically driven, ace helicopter mechanic of the most successful company in the entire regiment. When Joint Special Operations Command, or occasionally even the President, needed to activate a company for a black ops mission, they tapped the 5th Battalion D Company.

"Too late to run," John murmured in her ear.

"No. It's not. We drove from Fort Campbell, Kentucky, we can drive back just as easily."

"I'd be a goddamn pretzel by then."

She considered her options. The driveway in mid-June

was a tunnel of green that the setting sun was fast turning to gold. It was beautiful—and it was completely unnerving.

How could it be such a shocking contrast to the pure blue, winter sky she'd seen last December? She'd understood herself those three, cold winter days. Their bitter chill had fit her—an Army orphan. Those three days were the first she'd spent any time with a family since her slow-fading grandmother had died when Connie was sixteen. The first real family since her father had been shot down when Connie was twelve.

These lush fields and lovely farmhouse before her, so vibrant with life, were so foreign they could be alien. She didn't understand any of this at all.

A small figure in a bright sundress stepped out onto the porch. After shading her eyes, the figure waved.

"Now it's definitely too late," John teased her.

Connie had finally learned how to judge when he was teasing her with greater than ninety-four percent accuracy.

"Who's driving anyway?" She tried a riposte—which had less than a five percent success rate at stopping John, but she kept trying.

"Not you. We're just sitting our asses here. C'mon, honey. This boy wants to go home. That's Mama waiting."

"You're close enough to walk."

"Nope. Not giving you a chance to run."

"I won't." And she turned to look at him. How had she ever run from him the first time? He was such a good man and the way he looked at her, she could actually believe in herself. She had made the mistake of running away once—perhaps the greatest mistake in her life as it had almost lost her John. Never again.

"Maybe *I'll* be the one to get out and walk." And she'd take the keys with her if it would leave him stuck so close to home but unable to get there.

"Too late for that, too."

"Why do say thaaa—" She finished the last on a startled cry as a truck horn blared out close behind her. Only her seatbelt kept her from banging her head on the ceiling.

John waved cheerily out the back window.

Connie checked the rear view just in time to see Paps climb down out of his big pickup. He strolled up to her window with the rolling gait of a big man—almost as big and powerful as John—before crouching down to face her. They might not be related by blood, but Big John certainly *looked* like Paps' son.

"Getting pretty close to the altar to be getting cold feet." Paps' grin was as infectious as his step-son's.

"It's impossible to have cold feet during an Oklahoma summer," she did her best to smile back.

"Summer?" He inspected the sky in surprise. "This ain't but June. Even so, June brides got no excuses for cold feet. Do they, John?"

"Not as far as I can see, Paps."

"I was worried about you being the one with cold feet." The voice, and a smack on the back of John's head, came in from the window on his side.

CHAPTER 2

*J*ohn laughed and shoved the door open as hard as he could. It caught Tim Maloney in mid-crouch, knocking him head over heels into the corn.

"What are you doing here, loser?" John climbed out of the car.

They traded crushing hugs after Tim extracted himself from the stalks. "Figured you'd be the one likely to be getting cold feet. So, I flew in early to keep you in line. Paps picked me up. Tried to time it with your arrival. Good timing as always." He congratulated himself as usual. He and Tim had met in Basic Training and flown together for over a decade. He was the unofficial white-boy son in the Wallace household.

"Why in the world would I get cold feet?"

"Shit, bro, facing the big 'I Do,' especially with a hot chick like Connie? Figured you for a definite runner." Tim sent a wink to Connie where she was coming around the car.

She accepted Tim's hug, but John could see that she didn't quite know what to do with it. They were all Black Hawk crew chiefs for the 5D. Connie had earned her place—no one doubted that, not even Tim since their first Ukraine mission. But she was still…Connie.

"Hot chick" was the wrong adjective. That's what he'd always gone for in the past. Hot women, tall, and partial to short dresses revealing legs that went on forever.

He looked at his fiancée.

Connie was the classic sitcom-girl-next-door: quiet, unexpectedly pretty with the softest light brown hair in the world, and gold-brown eyes so big that they seemed both innocent and filled with wonder all the time. He'd seen her in a blouse and skirt a grand total of once. She was a camo pants and t-shirt kind of gal who barely came up to his chin. She was also absolutely brilliant.

He'd been the Number One mechanic in all of SOAR until she came along and showed him how it was really done. Together, they kicked serious helo ass. Command had already started asking when they were going to leave the field and join the airframe development team. Not yet, but it *was* nice of them to ask.

"Man doesn't get this lucky twice in a lifetime, bro." Tim tried to trip him, but John had been watching for that. "You get that shit, right?"

"Don't I know it." John turned to Connie, because he still couldn't believe a man could get this lucky even once. Out of the corner of his eye, John saw Tim's attention drift for a second. He casually hooked a foot behind Tim's ankles and shoved him back into the corn.

"Now don't you two go wrecking our crops," Mama slapped a hand lightly against John's shoulder before she stepped into his arms.

All he could do was hold on.

This was what home felt like, exactly like this. She smelled of the farm and his favorite peanut butter-chocolate chip cookies that she must have been baking pending his arrival. *She* was where he belonged.

Except that wasn't true anymore. He had two homes now.

And one stepped out of his arms to greet the other.

"Hello, Mrs. Wallace." Connie's shy setting was turned up full and he could see that her self-preservation blast shields were set for fast closure if needed.

"Oh, none of that now, Connie. Name's Bee and you know that right well."

"I do...Mrs. Wallace." Then Connie was actually the one to step forward into Mama's arms as Mama laughed.

John offered her an eye roll and Connie stuck her tongue out at him over Mama's shoulder. A very encouraging sign.

CHAPTER 3

*C*onnie didn't understand. She had learned to accept that there were some things beyond her, but still it rankled that some portion of her was simply...missing, and she couldn't even see what it was.

She had hurt this family and herself in the process—though being a loner since Dad's death when she was twelve, that latter part didn't worry her. And yet John's family treated her as if the only curious thing she'd ever done was to get engaged to John. She was made welcome at the big kitchen table as if she'd sat there a hundred times, not three. Her offer to help with the dishes had been readily accepted as if she was family, not a guest.

It was incomprehensible.

As evening had turned into night, they'd all moved out onto the porch to sip beers and watch the lightning bugs dance over the back lawn. The talk wandered as lazily as the big fans which dissipated the heat and the mosquitos. It focused on the news of the farm, mostly what was being planted where and why. With Grumps gone, Paps had taken full possession of his role as farm manager and head of the family. The family discussed the changes he was bringing in. Nothing big, but there were some crops that had flourished in Grump's youth that were no longer as viable with the changes in seed stock, the weather, and the marketplace.

She had grown up on Army bases and lived and breathed helicopters. It was all a foreign language to her, though she could feel through the arm draped lightly about her shoulders John's nods of approval about the changes Paps had made. Tim and Larry were farther down the porch trading girl stories.

"Girls and cars. Same thing every time those two get together," John whispered to her.

"Do you miss it?"

His low chuckle said that she'd been right, that was his earlier place on the porch. He turned enough to kiss her on the temple.

"Got the best girl anywhere already. Don't see much point in revisiting any past that glows less than a lightning bug when you're shining brighter than a sun."

"Smooth talker."

"Must be how I won your heart." It was anything but that. Smooth talk was almost as mysterious to her as why alfalfa was preferable to corn in the southwest acreage.

Connie had never imagined herself living long enough to think about a man in more than the briefest of terms. And the few times she did, she'd imagined a quiet, studious engineer. Instead, Big John Wallace was at the center of every story and launched every laugh that echoed through their flight crew. He lived in a state of innate joy that poured forth in his booming voice and grandiose gestures. It had pushed her away; made it clear that she didn't belong anyplace near such gusto for life.

But he'd won her respect by being the finest mechanic she'd ever met. Eventually he'd won her love by…seeing her.

By seeing her as she'd never seen herself; worthy of something more than fighting the good fight until some mission went horribly wrong and snuffed her out faster than one of the lightning bug blinks.

John, with a strong nudge from his sister, had given her a dream that lasted beyond the next mission. It was a gift she had never imagined.

He'd also given her a gift of family.

Yet another thing she still couldn't understand.

CHAPTER 4

"*H*ey, Knothead."

John eased open one eye to see his sister glaring down at him.

"Hey yourself, Meddler. When did you get in?" Noreen was six-months into her Army training as a medic and it clearly agreed with her. She'd always been slender and the real beauty of the family, but now there was a shine to her that came from being Army fit and loving it.

"Just now. Where's Connie?"

"What?" He opened his other eye and looked at the pillow beside him. No Connie, though it still bore the impression of her head. Barely. It had been smoothed out. He remembered the awesome wedding reception morning wake-up sex, but had fallen back asleep afterward. She had—

Run again!

"Goddamn it! She said she wouldn't!"

He jolted out of bed.

Noreen covered her eyes. "Whoa! Too much information, big brother."

John flipped the sheet around his hips and struggled to

reach his pants draped over the back of a chair while keeping himself covered, but it was tucked in too well on Connie's side. She'd, of course, made her half of the bed already—to full Army regulations—even with him in it.

"Ease the Code Red. Her gear is still here."

And then he spotted it. A small duffle bag, too small for any normal woman, but Connie wasn't normal. She was the queen of efficiency—even by Army standards. It still rested beside the dresser he'd meant to clear out for her last night, but forgotten.

He sat back on the bed with a gasp of relief. Noreen had been almost as devastated as he was when Connie had left the farm so abruptly on Christmas Eve after Grumps died.

"I'm going to forego the hug until you get yourself dressed. Mama has breakfast waiting."

He sniffed the air. Eggs, bacon, and her own warmed sand-plum syrup which meant pancakes as well. Pure heaven.

"You ready for this, Slacker?" Noreen dropped down to sit on his clothes, knowing full well she was delaying his race to breakfast.

"Look, Trouble. I can't get dressed if you're sitting on my damn clothes."

She raised her butt enough to pull out one sock and tossed it to him before settling back down. "Better?"

"Way!" He pulled it on just to show her who was in charge.

"So answer the question."

"What question?" He knew damn well what question.

That earned him yesterday's underwear in his face. He slipped into them under the sheet.

"What makes you think I'm gonna screw this up? I love her. I'm going to marry her tomorrow. Happily ever after will start immediately after the ceremony."

Noreen shrugged uncomfortably.

"What?"

"Don't know. Call it an itch."

"Shit. I'll track her down and ask."

Noreen scoffed at him just the way she used to when he'd bring a date home—one Noreen didn't approve of. It was her "You're so stupid" scoff. No way was he rising to the bait.

Or maybe he would. "What?"

"Don't you know anything about her? You hit her with a question like that and all you'll get is the blank mechanic look. You better let me deal with her if you want her to make it to the altar."

"You're saying you know more about my fiancée than I do?"

"Hello. *Woman* sitting here on your clothes. Can't help it. Besides, it's you. Larry's golden retriever knows more about women than you do."

"Can't you go bother Janice?"

"Oh, like I'm so close to her." Which was true. Of the four siblings, Janice and Noreen had never been close…at all. "But even she'd handle Connie better than you would."

"If I weren't still mostly naked, I'd whup your butt, Nori."

"I dare you to try. I double dare you."

John pushed off the bed to lunge at her, but she was too fast. Between one breath and the next she was gone out of the room.

When he turned to face the chair, he saw that his shirt and pants had gone with her. At least she'd left his other sock.

CHAPTER 5

"*H*e's gonna kill you." If John saw Connie leaning into the engine compartment of his pet GTO and tinkering, he just might. Even if they were engaged. He and Paps had kept it out in the barn and worked on it only when they were together. It had been one of their rituals since she was a little girl. It was never going to get done.

"Noreen!" Connie's look of delight was too big to fit on her face. And in the next instant, it disappeared back behind that ever-so-careful Connie wall.

"Hello! Happy to see you too."

"You really are?" Meek Connie asked carefully.

Noreen just laughed and hugged her. The fierceness of the return hug was shocking. It was very un-Connie-like. By the end of it, Noreen was discovering that she was feeling sniffly. Connie didn't hug her like her fiancée's sister; she hugged Noreen like they *were* sisters. Like twin sisters who had been apart for far too long, rather than two women most of a decade apart in age and who had met for three days. Three days that had ended in a funeral.

"I was so afraid that you'd be angry. I missed you so much," Connie mumbled.

"Me too." No matter how ridiculous, it was true.

Connie stepped back and leaned on John's precious car, shifting most of the way back into her usual self, though not all the way. No tears had run, but her eyes weren't any drier than Noreen's. There was a long silence as Connie gathered her thoughts, which Noreen had learned to wait through.

"And you've forgiven me for…you know?"

"Running out of here like a demon was chasing your ass?"

"Yes, that would be an accurate description. In several ways."

"Nothing to forgive. You're the one who finally convinced me I was doing something important and to hell with what anyone else thought." She tapped her collar where her lieutenant's bar would be if she was wearing her uniform. "I spend most of my days trying to figure out how to live up to *your* standard."

"My standard? I've spent the last six months trying to live up to yours."

Which set them both to laughing. Noreen knew so much about her, and also so little. It was awfully confusing. Which in Connie's neatly ordered world must be times a hundred.

So, Noreen sat down on an old milk crate in the corner.

"No! Don't!"

Noreen leapt to her feet and stared down at the crate to see if there was a giant milk snake or something.

"Sorry. I—" Connie studied the thin layer of straw on the barn floor.

"What?"

Connie just shook her head.

"Give, sis."

Connie eyed her carefully, "Promise you won't laugh."

Noreen crisscrossed her chest and held up a Girl Scout sign.

"When I rebuilt Grumps' tractor last Christmas, he would sit on that crate and watch me. I... It feels as if he's here with me if that crate is sitting there."

Noreen wasn't able to blink away the tears this time and soon they were both sniffling.

"He opened a hole in my world."

"Dying will do that. He loved you a lot, Connie. We all did. So fast."

"No, it wasn't his dying." Connie went over and straightened the crate so that it was angled just so.

Noreen could almost see him there—a big man that even age couldn't waste wholly away. His sparse tightly curled hair gone long past gray and into white. That easy smile that could welcome her home from a day at school as if she'd been away for a year or put her in her place with equal ease.

"It was his *living* that did it. He's the closest to family I've had since I was twelve."

"You're going to have a whole lot more tomorrow."

Connie offered a quirky smile, which was a new one on her.

"Maybe if I get this GTO running, I'll race out of here."

The car was in a kajillion pieces. The frame was there and most of the shiny black metal was back in place. And the engine was under the hood. But the hood was propped up against the barn wall and nothing was attached to the engine. Wires seemed to sprout everywhere. A stack of red leather interior panels were laid on a pair of sawhorses. The car itself was up on blocks with the tires sitting in the corner and no brakes or anything on the axles.

But if anyone could do it in the next twenty-four hours, it was her future sister-in-law.

"If you do decide to bolt, you've got to make me a promise."

"What?"

"Take me with you. Either that or I have to face a summer studying human anatomy."

"Deal!" They shook on it. "Can you give me a hand?"

And Noreen leaned in to work on the engine with the kind of sister she'd never had but always dreamed of. She didn't know a thing about engines, but she knew she was happier being close to Connie.

CHAPTER 6

*H*is plans to track down Connie—no matter what Noreen said—kept getting sidetracked.

Tim had been chowing down in the kitchen, which had turned into a long and friendly meal with Mama teasing them for being sleepyheads, the last awake. They'd all caught up with each other in ways they hadn't had time for last night.

As he finished washing the fry pan, Mama had given them a list for the grocery store, about a half million items long. So off to the local Homeland.

"It's weird buying groceries." John stared down the next aisle with some trepidation.

"How long since the last time you did this, man?" Tim asked as he stared wild-eyed at the cereal aisle. In an Army mess there were about five choices. At the normal forward operating base they were lucky to have a choice of one.

"A while," John glared at the list. Milk wasn't just milk, it was "two percent organic." Did that mean that only two percent of it was organic or... "Shit, man! It's been a long while."

"The Army provides."

It was strange. He hadn't had an apartment—ever. He'd gone from home to enlisted. Meals were dealt with. All kinds of civilian things were dealt with: no electric or water bills, no decisions about meals except whether to take the lasagna or the meat loaf. No question of even shopping at the PX for anything other than munchies, because no real point in keeping food around when you could be deployed on a moment's notice.

Connie had it even worse than he did, growing up as an Army brat. At least he could take care of this so that she didn't have to.

That didn't stop him from wishing she was the one stuck with this when they hit a produce aisle longer than the cargo bay of a C-17 Globemaster III jet transport.

"It's an issue, man," Tim agreed as they nosed their two carts into the vast array of greenery. "Feels like I'm doing an infiltration."

"It *is* an issue. How am I supposed to be the man of the family when I don't even know how to buy groceries?" Grumps had taken care of the farm into his eighties. Now Paps had taken up the reins and Larry would follow in his footsteps. Whereas he—

"Don't worry so much, bro. Connie is enough of a man for both of you."

He considered rearranging the lettuce display with Tim's head. She was certainly more woman than he knew how to deal with.

"At least she's not some weenie like you, Tim."

"Lame," Tim rated his comeback as they both stared at the carrots in dismay. The list said "carrots" but there was mini-peeled in a bag, full carrots in a bag, and a stack of loose ones two feet deep arranged in a neat stacked semi-circle with carrot butts facing them.

It *was* a lame response, but it was the best he had.

Tim pointed down the aisle to where there were more carrots still with their green tops and a sign above them that said organic. They finally took one of each kind of bag and a fistful each of the loose ones.

That's what they'd both always done: scooped up all kinds of willing ladies, had a great time, and let them go. Nobody pinned down Tim Maloney and Big John Wallace when they were in a target-rich environment.

"What the hell happened to me?" John stared at the eighty types of lettuce: head, bag, little plastic boxes marked spinach, or arugula. There were mixes, blends, hearts, and who knew what all. Even figuring out and eliminating the cabbages and cauliflowers (which took some doing) didn't narrow the target selection near enough.

"You stepped on the landmine of *luv.*" Tim drew out the last word like some British comedian.

He left the lettuce to Tim and moved down to potatoes. John had worked the farm as a kid, he understood potatoes. Russet, golden, red, mini, heritage...*Shit!*

The landmine of *luv* was about right. Every time he looked at Connie, it was impossible to look anywhere else. And when he touched her—

A hand rested on his arm. Long, fine fingers. He scanned up the tall, lean body into Jennifer's lovely face and even darker eyes.

"Johnnie," her soft voice evoking a thousand memories. They'd hooked up a number of times since their first real fling the night he'd quarterbacked the Muskogee High School Roughers to third in the state championship. If he was home on leave and she was between boyfriends, they'd heat up the dance floor at Clary's and then scorch the sheets.

"Hey, Jen."

"Didn't know you were back in town." Her hand still

rested on his arm. He knew full well how crazy she could drive him with those lovely fingers.

"Just a couple days."

"You know my number."

He could only nod. The words just wouldn't come out.

She sashayed away, picked up an apple and bit down on it with her perfect white teeth that could nibble at him until he was sure he'd died and gone to heaven. Sex with Jen had always been amaz—

Tim slapped him hard on the back of the head.

"What?"

"You did *not* just look at that." Tim's eyes weren't following Jen's walk around the end of the aisle, instead he was glaring at John.

"Some history there, man. Good history."

Tim smacked him again, and this time he looked pissed. "What the hell is wrong with you, man? Do I even know you? Marrying Connie Davis tomorrow. Sound familiar?"

John covered his face, trying to scrub the image of Jen out of his mind. She'd been gunning for him on and off for over a decade. He'd been looking for something different—never once imagining it was a short, quiet, white chick like Connie.

"Why is she scaring the shit out of me?"

"Jen? 'Cause she's the finest land shark swimming." When Tim had visited, they'd often double-dated with one of Jen's nearly-as-sultry friends.

"No, Connie." Jen had always offered an easy laugh and awesome sex. Connie had blown up his world and stolen his heart.

"Because you aren't stupid."

"You saying I'm stupid to marry Connie?" Normally those would be fighting words, but now he didn't even know.

"No, asshole. Smartest damn thing you ever did other than teaming up with me. I'm saying Connie is scary as hell.

She looked at you with those big golden-browns and, *Bang!*, you were off the market. No woman should have that kind of power over a man."

But she did. She totally did.

"You're next, buddy," he thumped Tim on the shoulder.

"No way in hell is some dame gonna pin down this boy."

"Yeah?"

"No. Way."

"Got a fifty on that?"

"Done!" They shook on it. He should have made it a hundred. "Double if it's inside six months."

"Yes! Easy money."

Then they turned together to face the question of onions: sweet, white, yellow, red, shallot... *Shit!*

CHAPTER 7

*C*onnie had most of the grease cleaned off in the shower. It would only take another couple hours to finish the GTO. She wanted to keep working on it, but Noreen had insisted that they had to stop.

"Reception dinner tonight."

"I don't have to go, do I?"

"It's for *your* wedding, sis-to-be." Noreen's smile had been merciless.

"But it *is* going to be small? Your mom promised."

"Small by Wallace standards. It's a farm wedding, been a long time since we had one of those, sis-to-be. Deal with it."

So, Connie scrubbed and worried. She wasn't good with people, but they seemed to like her anyway…eventually. And John loved her which was the only thing in her life that made sense. Why couldn't it be just her and John? They'd go back to his friend's steak house for dinner and make love in the USS *Batfish* submarine museum just as they had last winter. Then they'd—

"Now that's a sight I've been looking for all day." John swept open the plastic curtain around the tub.

He was so magnificent she couldn't speak. Stripped down, John was the most beautiful man she'd ever seen. Broad chest, powerful legs, and a smile that was all for her. She set aside the soap as he stepped in to join her. She wrapped herself around him as he closed the curtain and folded her against that lovely chest.

Here.

Here was where Connie the woman made sense—the only place. Her was where she came to life and the fears slipped away. She'd learned she could rely on that like her favorite 9 mm box-end wrench. John was her place of safety and security. A security she'd never known. Of all the people she knew, only John was even more reliable than a Black Hawk's T700 turbine, and even those needed care and maintenance.

Perhaps people were like that too. It was a reasonable hypothesis. She had spent much of the day with Noreen. Had she been teaching Noreen about electrical systems as they'd pulled new wiring through the GTO's frame together? Or had she been maintaining, even cementing their future sister-in-law relationship? Perhaps both?

She looked up to study John's face before she spoke.

"I love you, John." That she didn't say it often didn't make it any less true.

His smile bloomed as his eyes squeezed even more tightly shut. She now had a better understanding of his happy sigh that followed. She'd have to remember to say it more often.

She buried her face once more into his chest to reinforce her own happy sigh.

CHAPTER 8

*F*ive a.m.

No one in their right mind got out of bed at five a.m. Actually, that was usually around the time that a Night Stalker *went* to bed.

The house was silent. John knew Paps and Larry would be waking up soon, but they were working a farm. Even on a wedding day, the farm didn't wholly rest. They only kept a few dozen head of cattle for milk and beef, so the chores wouldn't last long. He wondered if he should wake Connie. Last night something had shifted.

They'd made love—a happy ritual they both enjoyed. Huh! He hadn't even thought once about Jen since she'd swayed away. Just thinking about Connie erased any other woman from even consideration. Being in her presence made it hard to think of *anything* else—like how comfortable his old bed was and how nice going back to sleep sounded.

Wasn't that a surprise? That a quiet, self-possessed woman could do that to him. Be funny to watch Tim when that caught up with him. John made a mental note to not give him the least bit of a break when it happened—and to collect his hundred bucks when some woman took Tim down for the now-and-forever dance.

But what was it that had shifted with Connie last night?

The sex had always been amazing. The contrast of such a careful woman who was so uninhibited in his arms was a constant wonder and being in the family bathroom hadn't changed that at all. He wasn't even sure who had taken who. Connie didn't play power dynamics—no question who was in control when he'd been with Jen. Jen had always made him feel like a man. Instead, Connie made him feel like he belonged exactly where he was.

Last night, after the dinner so rich with family and laughter, she'd simply held him as they lay together. She'd held him so tightly that it was impossible to imagine her wanting to be anywhere else. They didn't make pre-wedding love, they'd simply held each other in perfect, silent contentment.

Any worries that she'd run away again were simply gone.

He twisted around to look at her in the first hint of predawn light that trickled around the curtains...except she wasn't there. Her pillow was smoothed and her side of the bed was tucked in.

He turned on a light and managed to blink through the glare enough to finally see that her gear bag was still in place beside the dresser. Then where the hell was she? She'd eluded him all yesterday—not that he'd ever really had a chance to go find her.

A low rumble kicked to life somewhere out in the night.

A rumble that he'd imagined any number of times, but hadn't heard in forever.

It was a triple-carbed Pontiac 389 V8.

It was *his* triple-carbed Pontiac 389 V8.

John scrambled out of bed. The woman was working on *his* GTO.

In moments he was dressed and standing at the open

barn door. He'd arrived just steps behind Paps and could only stare aghast.

Connie and Noreen were sitting in the front buckets.

"Good morning. We were just headed out to the airport. Mark and Emily are coming in on an early flight." Connie dropped it into gear and rolled it out of the barn—the first time it had moved since he and Paps had pushed the aging rust bucket into the barn a decade ago. Now it was a black beast of a machine that shone with its perfection. He and Paps had hoped to finish it over the next couple times he had leave, but there hadn't been time to get near it this trip.

Connie and Noreen pulled on their mirrored shades against the sudden punch of the sun rising clear of the horizon.

Noreen waved happily as they pulled away.

"But—" he told the slight dust trail as the beautiful car and the two beautiful women spun away in a cloud of gravel and dirt.

Paps looked at him.

"I'm sorry, Paps. I told her last Christmas not to mess with it; that it was your and my project. She must have forgotten."

"Johnnie, you bring a mechanic into the family, you're going to have to live with the consequences. Besides, she asked yesterday if it was okay. Looked like she needed something to do. Just didn't think we were that close to done."

"We weren't. At least not for anyone less of a mechanic than Connie."

"Well, now that you're up, there's some milking and stall mucking to get done."

John's groan didn't save him. Begging off that it was his wedding day didn't seem likely to work any better. So, he followed Paps out to the cow barn and wondered at the miracle of a woman who had just driven away.

CHAPTER 9

*E*mily held out the suit bag as she walked up to the car.

"Thanks." Connie hadn't left it back at Fort Campbell intentionally. At least she didn't think so. Some part of her had been reluctant to think about the wedding? No. She'd been so worried about her lack of welcome at the farm that she'd forgotten about anything as trivial as the wedding and her dress uniform until she was halfway to Oklahoma. Simply a matter of memory stack overload.

Her commander had insisted it was no problem to pick it up when Connie had called. She still couldn't believe that Majors Emily Beale and Mark Henderson had come at all. She'd only given them an invitation because it seemed rude not to. They'd both responded yes immediately. Was it any wonder that the 5D was the best outfit she'd ever served with, having two such commanders.

"Your dress fits in there?" Noreen eyed the thin bag as Connie lay it flat in the GTO's massive trunk.

"My dress *uniform*. Easily."

"You're *not* getting married in your uniform."

Connie glanced over at Major Beale for support.

Emily shrugged, "I was married in a dress. So was Kee. But a uniform seems fine to me too. That's what I was going to wear before my mom brought a dress for me."

"So not!" Noreen looked furious.

"Well, I don't have a mom."

That chilled Noreen down several notches.

"All I have is my uniform." And it was enough for her. It always had been and it always would be.

"But the wedding is *all* about the dress."

"No, it's about marrying John."

"Aside from that," Noreen insisted. "It's *all* about the dress! My new sister is *not* going to marry my brother wearing a military uniform."

Connie thought they had come to a new understanding working on the car. And now Noreen was suddenly furious. What was wrong? Something spontaneous was going on that she didn't understand. Something bad was going to happen and she had no idea how to judge what it was.

Noreen yanked out her cell phone and dialed.

An airport patrolwoman came up and told her that they couldn't remain at the curb, this was a loading zone.

Emily and Mark settled in the back seat. Atypically, he was holding his peace and dutifully climbed in beside his wife. But nothing was going to move Noreen. She was as formidable as Major Beale in her own way.

Connie circled around the car, and pushed Noreen into the seat while she was waiting for someone to answer the phone. Connie circled back and offered an apology to the patrolwoman.

"She's right, you know. The dress...absolutely." Then the woman continued her patrol.

Connie slid in behind the wheel. She was just fine with

her uniform. It certainly defined who she was better than some dress anyway.

"Mama," Noreen yelled into the phone over the roar of a departing jet as Connie pulled them away from the curb and threaded back into the traffic. "Connie only brought her uniform. She doesn't have a dress."

...

"No, I don't think it's up to her. It's just not right. Where's a shop that we have a chance of finding something ready-made?"

...

"What do you mean 'just come home'? Didn't you hear what I was say—"

...

"Yes, Mama." Noreen snarled at her as she hung up the phone, "Just go home."

Between Noreen's mood and Connie's trouble speaking to Emily when there were other people around, the front seat was very quiet for the long drive back to the farm.

Once they were back at the farmhouse and introductions had been made, Bee Wallace shooed Mark away. "You'll find the boys and a cooler of cider and such around the back of the house. They're in the peach orchard."

Connie had fetched her uniform from the trunk and she stood on the ground between Emily and Noreen. Bee looked down at them from the top of the porch steps, fists on her hips.

"Well, miracle of miracles, my girl is right. You can't be getting married in a uniform. That's everyday wear, child."

"No, it isn't." Connie wore it for award ceremonies and not much else. She didn't get invited to weddings, was never anyone's date to a formal banquet. And it had no place in the field or hangar, which was where she was most comfortable.

"No matter. You just come inside and we'll get you fixed up."

Trapped, unsure of what else to do, she was herded inside between the women.

CHAPTER 10

"Iohn!"

"Hey Archie!" John greeted Archie as he came into the orchard.

"Expelled by the women?" Mark greeted their Air Mission Commander.

"No. I simply assessed that a male would be risking his life to so much as attempt entrance. Given an escape route, I deemed it the best angle of attack."

"To run away in full retreat!" Mark agreed heartily and handed him a cold beer.

"Damn straight."

Archie joined the circle.

Paps, Larry, and Tim were manning the grill—sipping beers and watching the charcoal slowly coming up to heat for lunchtime burgers because, well, someone had to. Mark and Archie dragged over a couple of the chairs from the pile they were supposedly busy setting up for the evening ceremony.

"How's he holding up?" Archie asked Mark.

"Shaking like a leaf if I judge properly."

"Am not." John's denial sounded unconvinced, even to his own ears. How could a man be nervous about marrying Connie? Just wasn't possible. No way. No how.

"Isn't easy, you know," Mark studied his beer. John noticed that though he been nursing it a long while, it was less than an inch down. God forbid Major Mark Henderson should ever lose the least bit of control.

"Nope," Archie agreed. His, at least, was a quarter down.

John set aside his empty quietly and didn't take another.

"We're all family men," Mark continued.

"Yeah, you're both married to amazing women." John couldn't argue that point. Emily and Kee? If he did argue, Mark and Archie wouldn't have to do a thing—either woman could execute him just fine on their own.

"You will be too, but that's not what I'm talking about. We all come from family. We know what it means. That's what makes it hard."

"Emily did too," John didn't know why he was arguing.

"Kee and Connie are both orphans."

"Couldn't find two more different women," John had a contrary streak going and decided to let it keep running. Archie's wife was a former street kid and a tough-as-hell outspoken sniper. But she had some kind of weird soft side around Archie and the Uzbekistani war orphan they'd adopted.

Unless...

"Did you two hitch up because of Dilya?"

Archie's look told him he was an idiot. No news there. His friend was sweet enough that he'd marry somebody if it meant protecting her. But that wasn't the point. There was no way to deny that Archie and Kee were electric together—like she was the explosive and he was the safety.

What did that make Connie and him?

Today, it made her the rational one and him the basket case.

"You're spooked because you get what family means," Mark concluded. "Connie doesn't."

CHAPTER 11

"*A*re you sure?" Connie could only look at herself in the mirror in astonishment.

Mama Wallace—impossible to still think of her by something as remote as her first name—had offered Connie her own wedding dress.

"For my future daughter, absolutely. Was I ever so slender and fine as you?"

John had showed her the photos. When she was younger, she could have been Noreen's twin.

The dress was simple and elegant. A loose-pleated sheath below the waist with an embroidered sleeveless top. It was in the softest pink with an only slightly brighter pink wide belt defining her waist.

"It's the dress I married John in, your John's father before he was killed by that drunk driver. I was so in love. We had less than a year together. I was too pregnant with John Junior when I married Paps to wear more than a sundress—which was okay, it took me time to learn to love him. But this is the dress of a woman already in love. Are you in love with my son?"

"Desperately." The spontaneous answer surprised her, but it didn't make it any less true.

"Then you are wearing the right dress."

Around her stood her new relations-to-be: Mama Wallace and Noreen. Also, the women of her team: Emily and Kee. Perhaps they were her old family? Had she already discovered family on a cold winter mission far behind Ukraine "friendly" lines, and somehow not realized it?

"Perhaps some day you'll lend it to your sister-in-law," Emily observed softly.

Connie looked at the shock on Noreen's face. Followed closely by the longing.

Connie reached out and took Noreen's hand. "A dress for Wallace women to get married in?"

Noreen could only nod. It was funny seeing Noreen unable to speak.

Looking back into the mirror, she knew it was right. She was about to become a "Wallace woman." Even though she'd decided to honor the memory of her father by keeping his last name, it wouldn't be the name of her children. They would all be members of the Wallace family. And if one was a girl, perhaps she too would wear this dress someday.

Dilya was there too. So ecstatic to be with "the women" that her limited English had mostly flown out the window. She made up for it by parceling out hugs at every chance. Spent for the moment, she leaned against Kee. Their looks came from completely different backgrounds: Uzbekistan and Kee's Latina-Asian mixture. But even the least glance couldn't hide that they were family.

Mama Wallace and Noreen, and soon Connie Davis. Two beautiful black women and a white chick. But she would be family.

Would her own children favor John's coloring or hers? It wouldn't matter, but she was surprised that she felt an eagerness to know. They had agreed that children still lay out in the future, after their service with the Night Stalkers, but she could almost see that future family. And in the present?

"I have a family *now*."

"Aw, crap!" Kee and Noreen sniffled together. Mama Wallace hugged her from behind.

Major Emily Beale softened just enough to smile at Connie's reflection. "I was wondering when you would notice."

"It's a new concept."

"Family?"

"No, having one. I've wanted nothing more than family since I can ever remember. My dad did his best, but he was often deployed six months at a time. With no mother, it left me to dream of family. But for all my dreams, I never actually thought I'd be part of one."

"Wake up, Sergeant Davis. You're about to become even more a part of one. Any nerves?"

"No." And Connie's reflection agreed with her. There was nothing she'd ever wanted more in her life. "I simply never believed it could happen to someone like me. But it already has."

Emily actually hugged her lightly, careful not to wrinkle the lovely dress.

"You're only just starting. It gets even better from here."

CHAPTER 12

*J*ohn stood before the bower made of two peach trees whose boughs joined above them in a graceful arc. Mid-June, the fruit was already ripening. The Wallaces had come from far and wide for the wedding. There were forty or more relations here, not counting the children who ranged across all ages.

Connie had so few people here.

Tim was here for him—currently asking John where the hell the rings had gone. No chance John was falling for that gambit, especially since he could see the boxes bulging in Tim's suit coat pocket. And Mark would kill him if he actually screwed this up.

Two female Night Stalkers for Connie was all she had in the world—their severe commander and the lethal Kee. His heart ached for her.

There would be more for her. He'd make sure of it.

That was a promise that he'd make on this day of promises and vows. He didn't know how, but he'd help her find family until she was surrounded by them. Until she couldn't turn around without—

First came Kee. She was in her uniform of course, leading Dilya. Together they sprinkled rose petals over the grass path that led into the heart of the orchard. They must have devastated one whole side of the house to have so many—pinks, oranges, reds, and golds scattered across the green orchard aisle.

Next Mama came round the hedgerow of sand plums that bordered the orchard. She looked elegant in a simple lavender dress.

He tried not to let his attention drift from Mama's hug and kiss, but he couldn't help looking to see Connie.

But it was Noreen who came next. She was crying despite the huge smile on her face. Noreen always was a mush.

Emily followed her, looking resplendent in her uniform—wearing far more medals than should be possible for any one officer to be awarded. She didn't say a word as she moved to stand to the bride's side beside Noreen. She didn't need to speak, her stare told him exactly what would happen if he hurt one of her crew. The fact that he was also one of her crew was completely irrelevant. Connie had helped save Emily's life and paybacks would be hell if John didn't live up to the expected standards.

Then he saw Connie turn into the far end of the orchard. John barely saw Mark holding her arm as he walked her down the aisle.

Connie was radiant. Her hair had been left loose, with just a light band to make sure it stayed clear of her lovely eyes. The sleeveless dress showed both her power and her impossibly feminine beauty. It was…familiar.

It was… He glanced sideways at Mama.

Her infinitesimal nod confirmed his guess. He had seen it many times in one of his favorite photos—his parents, his blood parents' wedding photo. He looked to see Paps' reaction—for Mama and Paps were his real parents as assuredly as if he was Paps' son rather than his nephew. His response was to wrap his hands around his wife's waist from behind and kiss her hair as they both looked back up the aisle. Mama hadn't been able to afford a nice dress for the wedding, and always said it was proof of how much John Senior had loved her for buying her such a dress.

And now Connie was wearing it along with a radiant smile as she crossed to him.

Mark kissed Connie on the forehead, just like a father might. Then he shook John's hand and threatened him in a whispered tone, just like a father would. Of course Mark's words were trite compared to Emily's glare. And both were meaningless in comparison to Connie's straightforward look.

His new wife's trusting look.

John looked at Connie's smile and those lovely wide eyes.

Their commanders' threats, his mother's gift of the dress, Noreen helping Connie finish the GTO, even Tim's leaping to be Connie's champion in the produce aisle. She already had family in more ways than he'd ever understood. And she knew it.

As they turned together to face the family minister, he could see his own family in a new light. Perhaps for the first time he appreciated just how lucky he was.

Then he looked once more at Connie and he knew *exactly* how lucky he was going to be: for as long as they both shall live.

TO READ CONNIE'S ROMANCE:

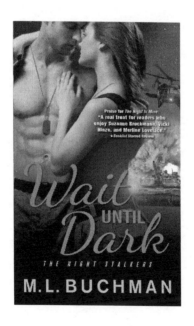

WAIT UNTIL DARK (EXCERPT)

*S*ergeant Connie Davis felt the metallic stutter before she heard it. It broke the rhythm of the music that usually floated in the background of her thoughts when flying.

She began counting seconds... four, five.

Again.

A third time to be sure.

"Major?" she called on the Black Hawk helicopter's intercom.

"What!" Major Emily Beale's voice made it damn clear that whatever Connie wanted had better be more important than the firefight going on all around them.

The copilot and the other crew chief, Staff Sergeant John Wallace, kept their silence. It surprised Connie that she'd heard it before Big John. He was the most amazing mechanic she'd ever met.

"We have," Connie estimated quickly, "about five minutes until lift failure. We're losing a main blade." And without that, ten thousand pounds of U.S. Army helicopter and her four crew members were going to fall out of the sky far too fast.

"You sure?"

Connie leaned out the left-side gunner's window to unleash another spate of fire from her minigun on the bunkered-in machine gun nest that was giving them such trouble tonight. A hailstorm of spent brass spewed out the window as she pounded sixty-eight rounds a second of tracer-laden hell down on the aggressors. More raw power than the cannons in Tchaikovsky's *1812 Overture*.

For the three long seconds that the nest was in her range, the tracer-green fire whipped and coiled across the sky like a nightmare snake. In three seconds she hurled two kilos of lead. Four and a half pounds didn't sound like much until you pumped it along as three thousand separate pieces moving at three times the speed of sound. She raked her flying buzz saw back and forth twice over the enemies' position in the time they were in view.

"She's right. Maybe ten minutes if you ride it soft," Big John chimed in. He might not have caught the problem, but as soon as she pointed it out he'd found the vibration rippling through the frame of the Black Hawk helicopter, had counted the seconds, and he knew.

It was her first time in full combat with him. But already he was a man she'd learned to really admire during training flights. A man she had real trouble not noticing. She kept finding herself watching him when he wasn't aware. Big John Wallace fully deserved his nickname and was also perhaps the most handsome man she'd flown with in a half-dozen years aloft.

That she was a step ahead of him would have been satisfying in any less hazardous situation. One look out the window was enough to wipe any thought of a smile entirely out of her mind.

Even at night, the Hindu Kush mountains of northeast Afghanistan looked ugly. And tonight's mission had taken their flight in deep, way past five minutes to safety, or even ten. Base lay forty-five minutes away, with four good blades, and the area around that ranked almost as unfriendly as the people shooting at them now.

They might be the Night Stalkers of U.S. Special Forces, the fliers who ruled the night. But if they went down here, they wouldn't be ruling the night for very long despite being the toughest gunship ever launched into the night sky.

"*Viper*, this is *Vengeance*." The Major, the first woman ever in the Night Stalkers, had long since proved her ability as a pilot and commander when fast decisions were needed.

Helicopters never flew alone into combat, and tonight's mission had paired them with *Viper*.

"We're losing a blade and running for home. Won't make it." Then she took one last turn, wide rather than her normal hard slam, giving Big John a final chance at clearing out the problem they'd been sent to solve. The copilot fired four rockets, and whatever they opened up, John drove home.

The shock wave hit them hard enough that Connie half feared they'd lose the blade now. ...Four, five, shudder, still right on cue. Okay for the moment. She puffed out a breath she hadn't known she was holding as the Major turned south by southeast.

They were through the smaller of two mountain passes while everyone on the ground remained distracted by the massive explosion that continued to roll skyward behind them. No one on the ground remembered to fire at the speeding helicopter until too late.

"Roger, *Vengeance*." The radio crackled in her helmet. "Heavy One is moving, thirty minutes."

Major Beale ran down the throttle to ease the load on the blade. They stayed low to avoid any stress from attempting a climb. That meant flying low through the next, very well-defended pass, assuming they didn't fold up and crash before then. Even with a good rotor, they'd already be up in high-hot limits. The combination of heat and altitude really knocked efficiency out of helicopters, the air was just too thin. With a bad rotor, they didn't dare climb out of harm's way.

The troops defending the pass less than a minute ahead were very unfriendly.

Connie thumped the ammo can with her boot, barely a quarter full. She opened her gun and tossed the ammo belt loose, snaking it back into the can. She snapped down the lid and pulled out a fresh belt from a new can.

Out of the corner of her eye she saw Big John, who sat back to back four feet away on the other side of the chopper's bay, making the same choice. Once again, they were in some sort of perfect synchronicity.

…three, four. Not good. She leaned out the window to spot the pass ahead. They were down in the gut of it. Open to fire from all elevations of both sides.

"Can I—"

"No." She and John cut off the Major in unison, almost making Connie laugh. No climbing, not on this rotor blade.

Connie switched on the night-vision goggles feature of her helmet. She'd turned off the NVGs to avoid being blinded by the rocket flare at the firefight. Now she needed any advantage she could find to see in the dark.

A wash of the world gone green projected across the inside of her visor. Leaning out the gunnery window to look ahead, she watched for the bright shimmer of gunfire or the sharp glow of running stick figures as fighters scrambled for position. They were there. A dozen or more. And several were higher than they were. She couldn't attack them, couldn't shoot upward, unless she wanted to take out what remained of their own rotor blades. Helicopters were designed to shoot down at things, not up.

"Major?"

"Stop asking and just speak!" Emily Beale was less steady than usual. Hard to blame her.

Connie swallowed hard and pictured it again in her head. She saw no better answer. It was either bet on the poor aim of the many gunners ahead of them or bet that the Major's reputation as the best Black Hawk pilot in all of the U.S. Army's Special Operations Aviation Regiment had been earned, rather than merely granted for being the first woman in SOAR.

"A roll is a neutral-gee maneuver." A slow barrel roll—flying straight ahead while rolling the copter over sideways, upside down, and back to right side up—actually placed very little stress on the airframe or rotor blades, if done correctly.

"Oh shit. She's right," John confirmed in that wonderful deep voice of his, making it almost sound rational even as the Major groaned.

Was it an act like this by some crazy or equally desperate pilot that had killed Connie's father? Why had she mentioned it?

"John, you'll be first. Then Connie."

Was this about to place her in the same unknown grave as her dad? Connie Davis. Just a name on the Night Stalker monument at SOAR headquarters. A short note in a secret file: Lost. Pilot, copilot, two crew chiefs. No survivors.

The Major aimed for the right-hand wall of the pass, almost head on. Moments before they would have hit the cliff face, the Major slewed the chopper back to the left. But not in a hard turn. In a long, slow roll.

The ground so close they nearly thumped their wheels on the rock passing at a hundred and fifty knots. At 175 miles per hour, death was only the slightest error away.

That was the moment Connie knew for a fact that Major Emily Beale had earned her reputation as the very best. Beginning the roll so close to the cliff wall reduced their availability as a target to those on either side of the pass. And it took advantage of the ground effect decreasing the stress on the blades. The Major had accepted the idea, planned the maneuver, and executed it all on fifteen seconds notice.

As the right side of the helicopter lifted, John's gun had a clear field of fire on the cliff face flashing by. He used the precious moments to rake the walls far and wide while Connie looked straight down at the ground racing by, going weightless in her seat.

They were so close that she watched the tips of the rotor blades swinging past sharp rock with bare inches to spare. She pushed back into her seat, her instincts taking control and trying to shove her body even another inch from impending disaster. The static electricity of the rotors striking dust in the air glittered in her NVGs, a green arc of brilliant sparks. So close to the rock, the sparks appeared to be inside it.

But with air-show perfection, the Major continued the roll, edging clear of the wall so that she didn't strike a blade. Now upside down, Connie had a disoriented moment to spot any fire John had missed. She only tagged one on the wall racing by so closely before she faced straight up.

In the moment of rolling silence, as she stared at the heavens, she recalled hearing John's gun fire just a few short bursts while they were inverted. That meant any remaining dirty work on the left-hand wall of the pass was going to be her issue as they rolled back to level.

Anticipating the moment, she leaned forward and drove down the triggers the moment she saw rock instead of sky. An arc of tracer-green fire poured from the six spinning muzzles. She swept her M134 back and forth as the chopper rolled, taking her aim at the cliff face flashing by in the night. Enemy rounds spattered against the airframe with sharp thwacks barely detectable over the roar of her minigun.

The threat detector flashed target information on the inside of her visor, and with instinct born of a thousand hours of practice, she swept the gun over position after position, cutting them apart faster than they could duck and cover.

And then the *Vengeance* was through the pass. The targets were falling astern at eighty meters per second.

Beyond the pass, the front range of the Hindu Kush mountains broke like a thousand-meter-high wave, collapsing in deep rolls and turbulent clusters. The flat horizon of desert formed in the distance.

…two, three. A distance they weren't going to make.

"Now, Major," John announced. There was no questioning the man, not when he used that voice. Six foot four and mountain strong with a deep voice to match. It was a wonder he could cram into the Hawk's crew chief seat, but he did.

Connie had never felt short, but the top of her head would fit under his chin, comfortably. Odd thought.

And he was right. Now, or they were going to fall from the sky.

"This is *Vengeance*. Going down. Repeat. Going down. Beacon hot."

It was a risk. Lately, the bad guys were getting their hands on night-vision gear. A lot of it was first-generation crap, but even that wouldn't have any trouble finding the brilliant, infrared beacon now flashing atop their chopper.

…One, two. The ground was coming up awfully fast. Connie glanced forward. Best not to interrupt the pilot at the moment, but she wondered at the woman's sanity. Major Emily Beale was a SOAR legend, but they were about to become just another footnote in the bloody history of the Night Stalkers. At her current rate of descent, they were going to dig such a deep hole in the desert that the sand might cover right over their impact crater.

Connie braced for the crash. This one was gonna hurt. And hurt bad. Assuming she was alive afterward to feel it.

Fifty feet up, she felt the shudder as the Major yanked the collective full up and cranked the throttle wide open.

Not crazy.

A calculated gamble.

The Black Hawk's twin turbines groaned in protest, then over five thousand horsepower roared to life. Connie heard them go right past redline, nearly six thousand. The blades howled in protest as they clawed the air like mad beasts. She and John chanting a mantra to the blade in unison, "Hang on. Hang on. Hang on."

Twenty feet. Ten. Slowing, five.

Then the blade let go. Twenty feet of laminated polycarbonate arced off into the night. Three blades remained, horribly unbalanced, but before they could turn twice more, the Hawk slammed into the sand. Not even hard enough to ram the shocks against the stops.

The Major dumped power, and the turbines collapsed from scream to cry toward moan. But not fast enough.

Another blade broke but didn't fly free. It slammed against the tail of the chopper, then the cockpit, then the tail again even as the rotor slowed. For ten seconds of held breath, they all waited while it dragged and beat the helicopter as it spun its way to a halt. The final scraping groan of wounded metal told Connie that half the bearings in the rotor head would need replacement and probably the swash plate as well.

"Everyone okay?"

"We're fine." Big John rolled free of his harness. "Now!" he called and snapped a monkey line to the steel loop by the cargo bay door.

Connie had to blink a few times. Was she fine? They weren't dead. They hadn't been killed by the failure of one of these hell-spawn machines. What next?

ABOUT THE AUTHOR

M.L. Buchman started the first of, what is now over 50 novels and even more short stories, while flying from South Korea to ride his bicycle across the Australian Outback. Part of a solo around-the-world trip that ultimately launched his writing career.

Three times, his titles have been named "Top 10 Romance of the Year" by the American Library Association's *Booklist*. NPR and Barnes & Noble have named other titles "Top 5 Romance of the Year." In 2016 he was a finalist for Romance Writers of America prestigious RITA award. He also writes: contemporary romance, thrillers, and fantasy.

Past lives include: years as a project manager, rebuilding and single-handing a fifty-foot sailboat, both flying and jumping out of airplanes, and he has designed and built two houses. He is now making his living as a full-time writer on the Oregon Coast with his beloved wife and is constantly amazed at what you can do with a degree in Geophysics. You may keep up with his writing and receive a free novel by subscribing to his newsletter at: www.mlbuchman.com

Join the conversation:
www.mlbuchman.com

Other works by M. L. Buchman:

SIGN UP FOR M. L. BUCHMAN'S NEWSLETTER TODAY

and receive:
Release News
Free Short Stories
a Free novel

Do it today. Do it now.
www.mlbuchman.com/newsletter

Made in the USA
Columbia, SC
01 October 2018